This book belongs to:

Mi Penguino
Adrián

For Mom and Dad.
—B.J.S.

immedium

Immedium, Inc.
P.O. Box 31846
San Francisco, CA 94131
www.immedium.com

Justin Time series, text, illustrations © 2013 Guru Animation Studio Ltd. All rights reserved.
Story based on an episode of Justin Time written by Bruce Robb.
Justin Time developed by Mary Bredin, Frank Falcone, and Brandon James Scott.
www.gurustudio.com

First hardcover edition published 2013.

Editor: Eric Searleman
Designer: Erica Loh Jones

Printed in Malaysia
10 9 8 7 6 5 4 3 2 1

Library of Congress Cataloging-in-Publication Data

Scott, Brandon, 1982- author, illustrator.
  The big pet story / adapted and illustrated by Brandon James Scott. -- First hardcover edition.
     pages cm
  "Story based on an episode of Justin Time written by Bruce Robb"--Copyright page.
  At head of title: Justin time.
  ISBN 978-1-59702-041-1 (hardcover) -- ISBN 1-59702-041-9 (hardcover)
  I. Robb, Bruce. II. Justin time (Television program) III. Title.
  PZ7.S41635Bi 2013
  [E]--dc23
                            2012043249

ISBN: 978-1-59702-041-1

# THE BIG PET STORY

ADAPTED AND ILLUSTRATED BY **BRANDON JAMES SCOTT**

immedium
San Francisco, CA

"Hey, Squidgy," says Justin. "Wouldn't it be fun to have a pet?"

"Yeah!" says Squidgy. "What kind of pet?"

I WANT the BIGGEST PET in the WORLD!

"What about a goldfish?" asks Squidgy.

"I don't know," says Justin. "A goldfish is kind of small."

"How about a hamster?" asks Squidgy. "Would you like a cat?"

The animals they imagine get bigger and bigger and bigger,
until Justin imagines the biggest animal of all...

"An elephant!" says Justin.

Squidgy wonders, "Where would you keep it?"

"If I were a prince, I'd keep it in my own palace," says Justin.

Just then, they see their best friend Olive standing at a splendid palace gate.

"Welcome to India, Rajah Justin!" says Olive.

"Hi, Olive!" says Justin. "What's a Rajah?"

"You're a Rajah, Justin! A Rajah is an Indian prince. I am the Rajah's royal pet keeper. I'll teach you how to take care of your new pet!"

"My new pet?"
asks Justin.

"Meet Tiny," says Olive. "Your new pet elephant!" A huge pink elephant stomps into the room and trumpets a great big "Hello" with her trunk. Squidgy giggles.

"Wow!" says Justin. "I've never owned an elephant before! How do you take care of it?"

Olive explains the rules.

**Rule # 1 – Elephants need lots of playtime.**

"To the royal playground!" shouts Squidgy.

The royal playground has a seesaw, a merry-go-round, and a slide. Everyone heads over to the seesaw first.

"Hey, Tiny, come play with us!" calls Justin. Tiny marches over to join them. She stomps her foot down and sends Squidgy flying into the air!

Squidgy thinks it's lots of fun.
"Hooray!" he shouts, popping into a parachute.
"Let's do it again, Tiny!"

Tiny stomps her foot again but
this time she snaps the seesaw in half.

SNAP!

That's ok," says Justin. "Let's take a spin on the merry-go-round!"
But Tiny is far too strong!

"Oops!" says Olive. "Why don't we hop on the slide instead?"
But Tiny is far too heavy!

"I don't think they made this playground for elephants," says Squidgy.

"What else do elephants need?" asks Justin.

"Elephants need to eat," says Olive.

## Rule # 2 - Feed your elephant lots of peanuts.

Justin pushes in a wheelbarrow full of peanuts.
"This should be enough food for Tiny!"

But Tiny sucks up all the peanuts as fast as a vacuum cleaner!

"Wow!" says Justin. "She sure was hungry."

"Yes," says Olive. "Elephants need a LOT of food."

Justin sniffs the air. "Hey! What's that stinky smell?"

"Uh, guys," whispers Olive. "Tiny left a little oopsie over there. We'd better take care of it."

"That reminds me..."

Justin grabs a shovel to clean up Tiny's mess.

"It's ok. Taking care of a pet is...easy-peasy," says Justin.

"And stinky-winky!" adds Squidgy.

Once Justin has cleaned up the oopsie on the floor, Tiny is happy again.
She gives him a big lick on the face and trumpets her trunk loudly.

"I guess she still wants to play some more," says Justin.

Olive gets Justin a leash. "It's time to take Tiny for a walk!"

# Rule # 4 - Elephants need lots of exercise.

Justin puts the leash on Tiny but she quickly charges ahead, pulling him all over the palace. Justin can't keep up!

"Phew!" says Justin. "All that exercise made me tired. I think I'm ready for a royal nap."

"You can rest in the royal bedroom," says Olive. But when they get to the bed, they hear a loud rumble.

SNOOORE

"Hey, who's asleep in my bed?" asks Justin. They look behind the curtain to see who's there.

It's Tiny!

"She's taking up the whole bed!" cries Justin.
Then Olive remembers another rule.

**Rule # 5 - Pets need naps.
Especially elephants.**

Justin sighs, "Well, I guess I'll have to sleep somewhere else."

Suddenly, Tiny bursts out of the bed and trumpets her trunk again!

Olive smiles, "Looks like she's finished her nap and ready for more fun."

"MORE FUN?!" shouts Justin and Squidgy.

"Are there any other rules, Olive?" asks Justin.

"There's just one more rule," Olive says.

# Rule # 6 - Repeat the other rules all over again.

"So that means..."

More playtime!

More peanuts!

More cleaning up!

More exercise!

And more naps!

"Whoa!" says Justin. "Taking care of a big pet is a lot more work than I thought it would be."

"Yeah," says Squidgy. "And I think we're out of peanuts!"

"That's ok," says Olive. "I have an idea. Follow me!"

Olive leads Justin, Squidgy, and Tiny out of the palace.

Before long, they arrive at the palace zoo. It's the perfect place for an elephant. It has a beautiful park with a pond, a jungle, and a zoo keeper who loves to take care of new animals.

Best of all, there's a new friend for Tiny to play with.

"How do you like it here, Tiny?" asks Justin.

Tiny trumpets happily. She'll have lots of elephant-sized fun here.

Justin and Squidgy are glad to hear that Tiny is happy at the zoo. Now they're ready to head back home.

"Bye, Olive!" says Justin.

"Bye, Tiny!" calls Squidgy.

"See you soon!" says Olive. Everyone waves goodbye.

Back at home, Justin says, "Having a pet sure is a lot of work."

Squidgy agrees, "But they sure are a lot of fun!"

"Hey, I know what would be a lot of fun," says Justin.
"Let's ask Mom and Dad to take us to the zoo!"

# The end.